Dizzy

AND THE DREAMS

Written by Marie Newton

Illustrations by Helen Cann

CHIRON PUBLICATIONS • ASHEVILLE, NORTH CAROLINA

www.ChironPublications.com

Illustrations by Helen Cann

Interior and cover design by Danijela Mijailovic

Printed primarily in the United States of America.

ISBN 978-1-63051-768-7 paperback

ISBN 978-1-63051-769-4 hardcover

ISBN 978-1-63051-770-0 electronic

ISBN 978-1-63051-771-7 limited edition paperback

Library of Congress Cataloging-in-Publication Data Pending

To Grace and Josephine Evetts-Secker...
for having a way with words.

CHAPTER 1

There was once a girl called Dizzy Woods. She was called Dizzy because she was pretty dreamy and preferred making her own fun. We usually use the word "dizzy" to describe someone who isn't smart; they never really know whether they are coming or going, and you can't rely on them. Dizzy wasn't like that at all; though she appeared to be. Admittedly, she had the habit of tripping over a lot, leaving her room in a mess and was mostly late to school every day. However, Dizzy's mind was different. She was incredibly smart but in a hidden, less obvious way.

She'd often wondered whether there was more to life than there appeared to be. This some-times aroused the jealousies of others around her. She liked to ask more questions. She wanted more answers than the average 12-year-old girl. Her dad died when she was seven years old and this had given her a longing to know more about the mysteries of life.

Dizzy preferred having her own space. She felt free that way. That way she wasn't being told what she *should* do, which left her room for what she *could* do. This day she returned home in the mood for drawing. Her drawing often aroused the envy of others around her too, so at home she was like an uncaged bird. At school, there had been too many text books and not enough art lessons. So after getting herself a snack and a drink, she escaped to her room and sat on the floor on her favourite rug. She got her pad and pencils out and started to draw. It just started with a scribble. Then it started to look like a forest. She liked rabbits...owls...pine cones...and imagined the smell of the trees. Well...she thought to herself, I would really love to go *there.*

She looked out of the window and thought to herself...I wonder what it is that's *between* me and that forest. If only I lived close to a forest instead of next to the convenient supermarket. Or if I could drive and have a car...yes it certainly would give me a few more choices. Dizzy liked the idea of *moving* to a forest. Her mum always spoke of how great it was living in a town, so convenient for cafes, restaurants and shops. Dizzy imagined being close to a clear lake, with unusual birds and creatures. She even imagined there was something more magical *there*. She thought maybe if there were another *kind* of world rather than this one, that it would be *there* rather than *here*.

She was just about to think about travelling there in her thoughts, since she didn't have a car, when her mum called her down for tea. Dizzy was very particular about what she liked to eat, and her mum knew it. Her mum was quite easy going, which she knew was better than some bossy parents. She realised that having the rules of school were enough for any child. She wasn't one for too much routine either, it didn't make for feeling independent.

So when she had finished her tea and got herself another glass of orange juice, she decided to get back to her drawing. *Something* was pulling her back to the picture. So she set back to it and decided that it needed a few people in it. She added a girl with a purple jacket, a boy with a blue jumper, a lady with a black poncho and a man with a white beard. Was there anything else she needed? Maybe a small house, somewhere to go and have dinner. Dizzy decided to make it evening time, *somehow,* the night seemed more exciting.

The blue, purple, black pencils began to run down so she had to keep her sharpener handy. The house, she decided, *had* to be wooden. It had to be a special house where you could feel important. Her mum shouted up that her favourite programme was on the T.V. but Dizzy was too absorbed in drawing her picture to notice.

Later her mum came to ask her to get ready for bed, but Dizzy had fallen asleep next to her picture. Her pencils had rolled onto the floor and her sharpener was clutched in her hand. Her mum smiled down on her and her picture. She moved the duvet over her and straightened it up. Her favourite toy was placed next to her head and the light was switched off.

Dizzy's sleep had taken her *into* her picture. She was in the forest with the squirrels, rabbits, pine cones and the lovely scent of the trees. At last, she was *there.* It was night time so she was a little afraid but decided that it was what she had wanted, and was too inquisitive to be too frightened. She crackled through the leaves and realised that she felt firmer on her feet than usual. She wondered which one was the real world...this one or the one at home. This world certainly *felt* different. And in a way, felt very real.

She was wondering about the *power* of drawing images when she heard a scuffling sound. Dusk was close by and from the corner of her eye she noticed a small, soft brown rabbit. It was nibbling at fresh green shoots and grasses. In and out of her sight slipped the rabbit and Dizzy wondered whether she could move a little closer without frightening it away. She carefully stepped closer and the rabbit noticed her. Instead of being frightened the rabbit seemed to be interested in her. He hopped closer and closer and she suddenly felt like she had a friend. She stroked it and it seemed to really like it. "Well, thought Dizzy, I'm not here alone after all."

What she noticed there was the stillness. She enjoyed the silent movements of the rabbit and that it liked to stay close to her. She preferred the *realness* of it, in comparison to watching TV and playing on her computer. She felt that maybe it was somewhere that she could *discover* things.

She walked further on through the forest with the rabbit and listened to the faint sounds of the birds, settling themselves into their twig laden beds. In the distance she saw the flicker of a light. She started to walk faster and faster to get close to it and the rabbit quickened its pace too. As she got closer she realised that it was a ladder. "Why's there a ladder sitting against a tree in this forest...very unusual?" she thought to herself.

She was *very* curious to know what was at the top of the ladder. She walked faster and faster to get to it. It was leaning against an extremely tall tree. Was it taller than the tree, she wondered. She wasn't sure. But she just *had* to know what was at the top. She picked up the rabbit, put it in her large pocket and started to climb. Ten, twenty, thirty steps...passing birds and insects on the way up. She got closer to the top. It got brighter and brighter, as though the night were turning into day. She was almost there. She got the feeling that you get when your plane starts to land in a foreign country. And sure enough, she wasn't just at the top of another tree, she was at the beginning of another world.

CHAPTER 2

The warmth of the sun touched her as she stepped out into what felt like another universe. There were animals, people, churches, castles, water pools, gardens and grand buildings. In the distance she could see the sea with a sandy beach. She took the rabbit out of her pocket and it happily jumped away by itself as if it were waiting to get back home. Dizzy was overwhelmed by all that was around her when suddenly a girl with a purple jacket said, "hello there, is it your first time here?"

Dizzy was shocked but at the same time relieved that she could talk to someone.

"Yes," she answered. "It feels like another world to me."

"Well, yes, it is," answered the girl. "My name is Phoebe, let me be your companion for the day."

"This is the *other* world," said Phoebe. "I only know this world, but occasionally we have visitors from your side."

"When you say 'your side,'" said Dizzy, "do you mean from earth?"

"Yes," said Phoebe. "I will show you around here and you can make of it what you will."

Dizzy was astonished and she thought of home and her mum and all the things she missed.

"Now," said Phoebe, "what is your name and place of residence?"

"My name is Dizzy Woods, and I was born in Whitby, Yorkshire."

"Thanks, now let's go and take you for something to eat. You must be hungry."

"Yes, I could do with some breakfast," said Dizzy.

Phoebe found her favourite café. It was a converted barn and had a very rustic feel about it. Some pancakes with blueberries were ordered along with fresh lemon drinks. The café had paintings by famous artists on the wall—Dizzy noticed one that her mum had at home by a painter called Kandinsky called "Accent en Rose." It was an abstract picture. It had kind of a square shape with lots of painted circles patterned inside and outside it. Dizzy liked the softness and the familiarity of it. She'd been looking at it at home the day before and *wondering* why she liked it. There were also lots and lots of books that were carefully ordered by subject.

"This looks a bit different to the cafes at home," thought Dizzy.

"This is the café that's dedicated to all the great *discoverers* who lived on earth," said Phoebe. "People who liked to ask questions, who weren't satisfied by the general rules of thought and behaviour."

Phoebe picked up a book on the subject of symbols and flicked through the pages. There were animals, colours, house-hold objects, all sorts of things. Dizzy liked the book and thought she might like to get a copy of it for herself. She saw lots of curious things to draw and read about.

"Is there anything in particular that you like in this book?" asked Phoebe.

"I like the bull," said Dizzy. "Everybody else seems scared of bulls, but I like them."

16

"They can be a bit ruthless," said Phoebe, "but they are certainly very powerful creatures. Let me take you outside and we can have a look around."

They walked out into the warmth of the sun. Dizzy looked by at a huge poster, on it was the artist, Salvador Dali. He was holding a red cloth in front of a bull as a matador, and his face looked a bit crazy. Then suddenly, the poster came to life. Dali moved the cloth in front of the bull and it literally jumped out of the poster. Dizzy's mouth dropped open and fear suddenly overtook her. The bull was coming towards them so they started to run as fast as they could. Dizzy had never run so fast in her life. They suddenly ended up being *somewhere* that looked strangely familiar to Dizzy. It felt uncanny. She saw a playground that really reminded her of the one at school. They *turned* a corner and the bull was gone. Dizzy and Phoebe panted for breath. Eventually there was a sense of calm after the exhilaration of the escape. They tentatively walked onwards. The playground was gone.

"Now," said Phoebe, "what could that mean?"

"What do you mean, what could that mean?" said Dizzy.

"Well, everything has a meaning in this world. It's a place of synchronicity. That means that something that happens on the outside comes because it coincides with something in our internal life."

Dizzy was slightly confused but decided just to have a think about what she had said. Phoebe seemed to know a lot of things, she obviously knew something that was mysterious about the place.

"Do you like to paint?" asked Phoebe.

"Yes, well, I find colouring pencils and felt tips a bit easier to use."

"Maybe you could *try* painting next time," said Phoebe.

Dizzy wasn't sure that she was good *enough* to paint.

They walked on until they got to the beach. They needed that feeling of tranquillity to digest what had happened. Phoebe got some drinks and an ice cream and they found a private spot to sit. She sat and thought for a bit and Dizzy was curious to hear what she had to say.

"Well, you know this happened after we had been looking at the book in the universal café.

You were interested in the bull. Here, in this world something always happens so we can learn something about ourselves that we didn't know before."

Dizzy was getting more and more interested.

"You mean to say that it happened because I was interested in the bull in the book?"

"*Yes,* that's exactly right," said Phoebe. "*Something* drew you to the bull. All the images from the book are symbols. They are from the collective library of the mind that we draw on when we need help. They are not from our own mind, they are from the collective mind. They are there to help us develop and become who we are meant to be. They help us to grow and live our life to the fullest. They help us to find ourselves."

"What has the bull got to do with me?" said Dizzy.

"They can symbolise power, energy, creativity and the drives of the human being. That bull wouldn't have hurt you. It's a part of you that you're a bit unsure of because it is a strong instinct. Next time, turn around and ask the bull what it wants of you," said Phoebe.

Dizzy wasn't sure that she wanted to turn around and ask the bull what it wanted. It might not end well. Her mind was on overdrive...what did the bull want, why was it near the playground, how did Phoebe know how it might react? And anyway, what did she mean a *part* of me? And what did Salvador Dali have to do with it? Despite all these questions, Dizzy could feel the blood running through her veins and a nervous excitement that she hadn't experienced before.

CHAPTER 3

Dizzy suddenly felt energised. Then she heard the sound of her alarm clock. It was 7 a.m. and time to get up to get ready for school. She pulled herself out of bed and looked out the window. The trees seemed a bit greener, the sun seemed to make her happy and the birds felt like they were calling to her. She thought about her dream and wondered what it all might *mean.* She looked at the picture she had drawn and wondered how on earth she had entered into it when she fell asleep.

She rushed to tell her mum about it.

"I had a dream mum, it was so vivid and so real and I met a girl called Phoebe. It was a wonderful magical world...do you think that dreams really mean anything?"

"Yes," said her mum. "They are important and we can learn a lot about ourselves from them. It's good to write them down so we don't forget them. I'll buy you a diary if you like and you can keep it for your dreams."

"Thanks mum, yes that would be great."

Dizzy went to school with a spring in her step that day, looking forward to seeing her best friend Alice. When she got there everybody was getting ready for a trip out to the local pond. It was a nature lesson and they were all told to change into their wellies. A day out was certainly better than being stuck in the classroom.

"Could everybody make sure they have their fishing nets to take to the pond?" said Mr. Tewksbury. "We don't want anybody being left out."

They set off down the lane. It was a beautiful day and the sun was glistening through the trees.

"I wonder what we will see today," said Alice.

"Who knows, maybe some unexpected creatures," said Dizzy as she floated along the road.

"You're the unexpected creatures," said Nicola, the class bully who was always ready to put the girls down with critical words. Scoffing, critical words.

"Very funny," said Dizzy, who walked faster to get away from her interference.

"I wish that Nicola would stop all those 'put downs.' I've had enough of it," said Dizzy.

"She's just jealous," said Alice, who always seemed to say the right thing at the right time. Along they went down the leafy lane. They breathed in the fresh grassy air and it seemed to infuse them with new life. At last, they reached the pond. They felt far away from everywhere.

The children positioned themselves around the pond in a circle. There was giggling and excitement but Mr. Tewksbury reminded everyone that there needed to be quietness so as not to scare the fish and pond creatures away. The silence was audible.

"It feels almost like the other world," thought Dizzy to herself. She hadn't dared tell anyone about her dream, apart from her mum. It felt too sacred, and that something might get broken once it was out in the open. So she kept it secretly to herself, even though this was difficult for her.

The children sat patiently around the pond with their fishing nets dipped into the dark brown-green water. There was the damp smell of pure earth and water combined mixing and transforming the mood of the atmosphere.

"This is much better than being in school," said Dizzy.

"I know," said Alice. The freedom was the kind of freedom that children crave but don't always experience. The girls felt a natural connection with the earth.

"I think I may have caught something," said Dizzy, as she pulled out her net. "It's a tiny fish." She lifted it up and then lowered it into her bucket of water. It quickly shimmered its way around in its new water. It was slim and silver and charged with life. Other children started to pull things out of the water. Some found tadpoles, others found dragonflies and pond weed. Alice found a tiny frog and was very pleased with herself.

As they walked back to school with their treasure, Dizzy wondered what Phoebe in her dream might think of their day out to the pond. She had an *urge* to tell her, even though she thought that it was *only* a character in a dream. She walked wistfully, thinking of the other world.

"You two should have stayed at the pond," said Nicola, "...with the slimy pond life. You'd feel at home there." She smirked and marched past to be at the front of the line of children.

Dizzy sighed at the comment and felt dragged down again but knew that people who were like Nicola could only feel good when they put others down.

"Low self-esteem," said Alice. The girls looked at each other and smiled.

Dizzy returned home from school with her tiny new fish. She went into the back garden with her mum and carefully lowered it into her own pond.

"Beautiful," said her mum, "a new addition to our own pond."

"Yes," said Dizzy, "and a new companion for the other fishes."

Dizzy meandered around the garden...she liked to wander around by herself sometimes. She drifted past the flowers and shrubs, in and out of the nooks and crannies. She found her sand pit in the centre and sat down with all her favourite objects. There was a prism, a castle, an emerald coloured stone, a tiny crystal ball and lots of pebbles. She liked to arrange them in different ways. Time seemed to disappear when she would play in the sand. She was absorbed in making different arrangements and patterns. She liked to be *alone* in her sandpit...it seemed to feel better that way.

Her mum eventually called her in for tea. She breathed in the tomato and basil sauce as she walked through the kitchen; the familiarity of the aroma was comforting. She sat down to her meatballs, tomato sauce and spaghetti. Garlic bread was brought out of the oven and her mum sat down to eat with her. Dizzy dipped her garlic bread into the sauce and it tasted like heaven.

"I wish I could cook like you mum...you always make things taste so good."

"That's just years of practice," said her mum. "You will be able to cook your own food one day." "I bought you a diary today...it has blank pages so you can draw in it as well. I thought you might like to draw your dream images too."

"Thanks mum, I was hoping that you would remember to get it for me."

As the evening was drawing to a close, Dizzy decided that she would squeeze as much out of it as she could. She went to her room and looked at her picture. She was curious as to how her mind had taken her into the picture on that strange journey.

"How did that happen," she wondered. "I certainly didn't *make* it happen."

She decided to draw another in her new diary. This time she started with a golden ladder. Then at the top of the ladder a dividing line and above she drew a sky. She decided that it was night-time and that the dark sky was full of the most beautiful bright stars. There was the outline of a bull in the sky—like a dot to dot. She knew that there was a constellation of stars in astronomy in the shape of a bull. A tree was placed in the foreground where a large owl sat at the top looking perfectly poised for the night-time activities. She added a small dark pond and last of all, the moon was placed in the top right corner of the page, beaming and yellow, shining its light into the pond.

She put her pencils down and got ready for bed. As she shut the curtains she looked out at the night sky, she saw the bright stars glimmering and the moon with its luminous glow. She wondered why we had to have a day and a night instead of continuous time with the odd nap in between. She felt somehow comforted by the night sky and decided to leave her curtains open. As she lay in bed she looked towards the window once more before sleep took her *somewhere* else. The light from outside shone down on Dizzy, as she drifted away into sleep.

CHAPTER 4

Again she was in the forest. A wave of feeling came over her, the same feeling that she had felt on the first visit. It was the kind of feeling that was satisfying, like having a new set of glasses that can suddenly allow you to see clearly where previously it had been a bit hazy. She walked through the forest and listened to the sound of her own feet crunching over the forest floor. She noticed the glimmer of something in the distance and saw the familiar ladder. *But* this time it was golden. She started to walk faster; she was curious to get to the other side and find out more about that other world.

Dizzy noticed that the rabbit was following her. She squealed with delight and put it in her large pocket. She placed her foot on the first rung of the ladder and started to climb. She felt her body pulling her to the top. She finally reached the top and again it was bright and the air was fresh with a soft breeze. She took the rabbit out of her pocket and set it free. It hopped away happily in its other home.

She looked around hoping to find Phoebe somewhere close by. She couldn't find her anywhere. Instead a boy with a blue jumper tapped her on the shoulder.

"Hello, my name is Paul. I'm going to be your assistant for the day."

"O," said Dizzy, taken unaware. "I wasn't expecting to see you, I thought I might bump into Phoebe."

"It's always a bit unexpected around here. She's out somewhere else at the moment, and I'm here to help you on your travels. Let me take you on a trip down to the lake. We can take a boat and have some lunch."

"Thanks," said Dizzy. "That sounds good." She felt a little apprehensive but at the same time excited.

Paul took the lead and bounded downwards towards the blue and green lake. He seemed to be very sure of himself and Dizzy felt quite over-awed by his presence. They picked up food for a picnic lunch to take onto the boat. They got down to the lake and Paul marched towards his fishing boat that was roped up. He masterfully unwound the rope and jumped into the boat. Then he took Dizzy's hand and she tentatively stepped on board. Dizzy wondered what her mum might think of her going out alone with a boy she'd only just met. And on a boat. But then she quickly forgot and her senses started to enjoy the sway of the boat and the pattern of the water as it moved through the lake.

"What a beautiful day," she said, as they sat together.

It felt like the most normal thing in the world. They glided around the edge of the large lake and Dizzy looked at the birds fly in and out of the trees. Paul seemed happy rowing the boat and being her guide for the day. She took out the picnic and they ate as they travelled. It seemed like the perfect way to spend the day.

Eventually, Paul took out his fishing rod and gave Dizzy a rod too. They sat for seconds, minutes, half an hour...the time just seemed to go by. Paul's rod started to bob up and down frantically, and all of a sudden out came a fish that was big enough to eat for supper.

"Wow, what a catch," said Dizzy. They both were giddy with excitement.

"It was worth the wait, hey Dizzy?"

"Yes, certainly was," she replied.

He unhooked the fish and put it into a water-filled bucket. Again, they sat expectantly, waiting for another catch. Then suddenly a strong wind blew the boat and it started to rock. Paul held the bucket as steady as he could to keep the fish from jumping out. Dizzy pulled in her rod and to her surprise pulled out a large question mark! What on earth….

CHAPTER 5

Dizzy woke up to her 7 a.m. alarm. She was in a suspended state, trying to work out *why* she had fished out a question mark of all things. She rolled out of bed and pulled out her uniform from underneath a pile of toys and magazines. She was half here and half there. As she put her dress on she was full of the feeling of the other world.

"I wish it was a bit easier to understand," she thought.

It seemed like an important puzzle that needed to be solved. She tripped over a jigsaw she had started and made her way downstairs for some toast and tea.

It was Saturday and the start of a half-term break. Dizzy's mum decided that they were due a trip to the city of London. So they got their things together to take a long weekend in Covent Garden. Dizzy loved the market there and the street entertainers. The trip was long and took hours, but they both liked travelling on trains, going from one place to another. Dizzy sat and read magazines, drew some pictures and started to write in her new diary. After she had finished her reading, writing and drawing she looked up and out of the window. Fields, trees, houses, buildings all went by and her mind relaxed. She liked the sway and sound of the train as it moved from *here* to *there.*

They arrived at Euston station and Dizzy was ready to explore. Walking towards the underground station they took the escalator which took them down underneath the station. There were many people, everyone busy with somewhere to get to.

At last they reached Covent Garden. Instead of taking the lift they climbed three hundred steps and by the end of it they were both ready to drop. Her mum found the hotel and they were glad to take the lift to the right level. At last, they reached their comfortable room. It was spacious and bright and Dizzy felt different. The kind of different that she felt in her dreams. There was something exciting about being in a different place and not quite knowing what was going to happen.

Her mum sensed her curiosity and said, "Right, now we are here shall we go and have a look round and find a nice restaurant?"

"Yes," said Dizzy, "sounds good to me."

So they showered and got changed and headed out into Covent Garden. It was colourful and vibrant and Dizzy loved it. There were street entertainers—people just dressed as different characters. There was a Victorian lady sprayed with silver, a Jack-in-the-box, a Mr. Bean look-alike and a witch with a very large nose and a green face. Dizzy had taken her camera out with her and managed to get some great "Selfies" with the different characters. Her mum looked at her amused, proud that she could just go up to people and take a photo with them if she wanted to. She realised that her daughter was getting more self-confident.

Dizzy's favourite food was Italian so they hunted down a perfect little restaurant. There were little tables with checked table cloths on them and a little candle on each one. The smell of garlic and herbs filled the air and the friendly waiters made them very welcome.

"This feels like being on holiday," said Dizzy.

"Yes," said her mum, "a multi-cultural city can make you feel like that."

The food was served and they tucked into their feast; it was a feast good enough for a king. They talked about what they might do the next day and they decided they would look around the galleries. Having the meal made them feel satisfied and content. They headed back to their hotel and Dizzy admired the pretty street lamps as they strolled along.

Dizzy was glad to be in London, it was so different from home. She certainly loved the beauty and tranquillity of Whitby, with its quaint lanes and cobbled street atmosphere, but a trip to London was what she had *craved* for. Just going there a few times a year made it more special too. As she walked she wondered what the place might have looked like a hundred years earlier.

This made her think about what her ancestors might have done too. What did they look like? Was she like them? Did they have the same thoughts as she did? She wondered whether their thoughts and aims might be passed down to her; passed down for her to work out. She didn't ask her mum these questions, it was getting late and time for getting her pyjamas on. She snuggled down in a cosy comfortable bed with feathered pillows and fell asleep.

CHAPTER 6

Again, Dizzy slept herself into the forest. This time she ran through the trees to get to the ladder. An urgency was within her and a force helped her move quickly. She took a quick look behind her and noticed there was an old woman following her. The woman was running after her and Dizzy felt her blood racing through her. She was running very quickly for an old person. Dizzy tripped over on a bush and struggled to get up quickly enough. The woman at last caught up.

"What are you up to little girl?" she said in a creaky voice. "Are you looking for the ladder?"

"Yes, I am," said Dizzy. "'I'm trying to get to the other world."

"It's not there today," said the old woman. "Sometimes it gets taken away."

Dizzy's heart sank. She was afraid. She didn't know where to go and she wondered how she was going to get away from the old woman.

"This is my wood," said the old woman. "Come and see where I live, I will take care of you while you are waiting for the ladder. I have some jobs that you could help me with while you are waiting." Dizzy felt that she had no choice. She wondered whether she had been caught in a trap.

She was guided to a wooden house deep into the woods. It felt silent and there was a darkness about the house that caused Dizzy to freeze inside. They went inside and Dizzy was asked to sit down on a bench. The old woman took off her black poncho and hung it up behind the door.

"Could you put the wood in the fireplace and light it for me?"

"Yes," said Dizzy, not really knowing how to light it but too scared to ask. She managed to throw some chopped logs into the fireplace and found a lighter. She lit the fire and sat down, relieved that she had managed to complete the task.

"I could do with a young girl to help me. I'm getting old and need a pair of fresh eyes and hands to do some housework for me."

"Yes," said Dizzy, "I will help you with it but I will need to get back by tomorrow."

"We will see," said the woman. "If you do what is required of you, I will let you go."

Dizzy felt herself go cold and looked around to see if there was a way out. The woman had a fox that guarded the door and her heart sank.

"My old attic room needs a good clear out and decorating. Yes, it needs the cobwebs cleared and a good dusting and painting. I will choose the colour. I like red. This room will suit red. If you do that for me I will give you my fox as your companion. If you decide that you can't be bothered, he might just turn nasty on you and you'll never get back to the other world."

Dizzy never expected there to be a dark side that may stop her from getting to the other world. The only thing that had ever made her feel this scared was when she lost her dad; it had made her feel that there was an emptiness that could not be filled. The room felt like this emptiness. She looked around at the bare wooden floors and the dusty window panes and her heart sank. The old woman had left several tins of paint and some brushes.

Dizzy prized the lid off the red tin. She stirred the paint around with the handle of one of the brushes. She remembered her dad doing this before he started to paint walls. She dipped another brush into the paint and started to paint the wall with large strokes. The colour reminded her of the colour of blood and although she felt a heaviness, she felt a relief from the act of painting. She got into a rhythm and forgot about the slowness of time.

She *wondered* about the power of colours and how they can make us feel. She pondered on whether they were a part of us, like another mysterious sense. Suddenly, as she was painting the wall, words started to appear by themselves. Dizzy stood, with her mouth open, not knowing what was happening. The words "lost," "empty," "confused," "angry," "pain" made themselves appear. She felt shocked and sat down on the floor. She had to close her eyes and try and absorb what was happening. She felt the room spinning. The words "disorientation," "dis-sociation," "despair," appeared. She opened her eyes but had to close them again. Dizzy started to cry and felt lower than she had ever felt. The meaning and force of the words came toppling down on her; from the top of her head right through her body down to her toes. She sat for a few minutes with her hands covering her face.

Her cheeks were wet with tears. She opened her eyes and the words had disappeared. The tension inside her subsided and a calm came over her. She looked towards the window and saw a face appear *through* the window. It was the face of her dad and he was smiling at her. Dizzy rubbed her eyes, but his face had faded away. *Nevertheless,* his appearance had caused a wave of peace that filled the room. Dizzy had felt his presence and that was all she needed to continue her task. A light shined through the window and permeated the room.

She decided to open another of the tins of paint. She liked the blue. She mixed the blue and red together and it turned into a beautiful violet colour. She found another large paint brush and started to paint the wall violet. Her energy started to soar and she raced through the room, layering the colour all over the walls. She didn't fear the witch because she felt that her dad was looking after her, guarding her as she did it; *inspiring* her in some mysterious way.

As she was close to finishing the room she wondered about the afterlife. "There must be life after death, I'm sure of it now." After having the thought she heard a scratching noise against the door. She opened the door and the fox looked at her and came into the room. Dizzy didn't know whether to be frightened or happy at the sight of it. The fox rubbed up against her leg and she realised that it was safe. It scratched at the floor and she realised that it was trying to show her something. There was an opening with a latch on. Dizzy opened a secret door and saw that there was an escape tunnel that burrowed underneath the house. She could hear the voice of the witch in the distance and her heart started to pound. The fox quickly jumped through the floor opening and she followed on. She shut the floor door behind her and heard a screech from the witch; the sound pierced Dizzy right through to her bones. They ran and ran through the dark tunnel. The tunnel came alight with stars and she could see a light in the distance and a wave of relief came upon her. She had escaped the witch with the help of the fox— her friend and rescuer.

CHAPTER 7

Dizzy opened her eyes and found herself in the hotel room in London. The dream had moved her to silence and her mum wondered whether everything was ok with her. She reassured her mum and got herself ready and went down to the restaurant for breakfast. She thought about the witch, the red room and the vision of her dad. She knew that something had changed within her and that a deep place had been touched. It was as though the rain had cleared her inner soul. She wondered whether there was something powerful that created her dreams; something that knew more than she did, something from *another* world. She didn't want to worry her mum with all of this, so she thought she would think more about it later.

They chatted over breakfast about what they might do in London. Dizzy liked the idea of going to the Tate Modern gallery so they decided to make a day of it. The breakfast helped them to recharge their batteries and they *set forth* towards the Tate.

The building was large and imposing and Dizzy wondered about who might of decided upon such a gigantic modern building. The first room they walked into had enormous Mark Rothko paintings hung on each wall. There were reds, blues, purples, oranges, blacks and browns. The artist had just painted large canvases of colours, nothing else. Dizzy was overwhelmed by feelings; even tears arose in her eyes. She had not expected colour to make her so emotional; but it did. She kept her feelings to herself; it was too personal, even to tell her mum. The final painting she saw was red and violet and she stopped and stared at it for a minute or two and drank the colours i *in*

She had begun to feel hungry and asked her mum whether they could go to the café. They searched for it and found it on the next floor. It had little white tables with a red flower on each one. Dizzy chose some pancakes with blue-berries and a lemonade. She thought they were delicious and that she could eat them all over again. She was excited and her mum knew it. They decided on a visit to the top floor and found a room where children could draw if they wanted to. Dizzy felt like painting.

They took the lift and walked to the next gallery and were surprised to find there was a Salvador Dali exhibition. Dizzy felt a cold shiver go down her spine. She thought of her dream with herself and Phoebe being chased by the bull and then recognising her school playground close by. There was a black and white photograph of Dali looking straight into the camera – he certainly has his own individuality, thought Dizzy. He didn't really care about what other people thought, he was truly himself. She thought he had a great imagination. She read through the information about him and found out that sometimes he would paint his own dreams.

Dizzy found the art room for kids and set to work. She didn't really know where to start. She looked around the room and saw a quotation by Van Gogh: "If you hear a voice within you say 'you cannot paint,' then by all means paint and that voice will be silenced."

She picked up a paint brush and looked at it. She was given a large piece of paper and wondered *how* the space was going to be filled. She took a pencil and tentatively drew the outline of a large body. It was neither a man nor a woman— just a human being. She looked at the different paints and decided on black. She painted the figure and concentrated on filling the paint in between the lines, making sure not to go over the edges. Then she gave her brush a good wash, until all the black paint was washed out of it. Then she dipped the end of the brush into silver paint. She painted stars into the picture of the human. She left it to dry and decided to return to it later to take it home with her. So off they went, strolling around the different levels of the gallery.

Once they had seen every level they decided to go and pick up Dizzy's picture. She felt pleased with it, painting it made her feel complete, like something had been solved. They walked back and found the tube station that would take them back to Covent Garden.

The day had been full and they were both tired, so they headed back to the hotel for one last night. They ordered a pizza by room service and decided to watch the film "Beauty and the Beast" on television. The Beast was certainly fearsome—he wore long blue coat tails and had a magnifying glass balanced in one eye. Nevertheless, after starting off bad-tempered, he took care of Beauty like a gentleman. Eventually, her heart softened towards him and Beauty's tears broke the spell of the curse that had turned him into a beast. The Beast had been rescued by love before the rose had died. Dizzy went to bed feeling content with the ending of the film and her mum read a poem to her as she drifted off to sleep.

Slowly, silently, now the moon
Walks the night in her silver shoon;
This way, and that, she peers, and sees
Silver fruit upon silver trees;
One by one the casements catch
Her beams beneath the silvery thatch
Couched in his kennel, like a log,
With paws of silver sleeps the dog;
From their shadowy cote the white breasts peep
Of doves in silver feathered sleep
A harvest mouse goes scampering by,
With silver claws, and silver eye;
And moveless fish in the water gleam,
By silver reeds in a silver stream.

By Walter de la Mare

CHAPTER 8

The beauty and atmosphere of the poem transported Dizzy into her dream with its magic. She had felt the silver touch her soul *somewhere* deeply. The forest was quiet and calming as she walked the familiar path that took her to the ladder. She breathed in the winter air and a gentle snow began to float through the air. There were snow flowers too, each with a beautiful pattern of its own. It was early enough just to see the moon disappear back beneath the clouds.

Dizzy climbed the ladder and as she was nearing the top, she could see an old man waiting for her at a turn style. He looked gentle and wise and had a long white beard.

He said "Good day" to her and handed her a golden coin and a warm coat. She thanked and nodded to him in respect and appreciation, passed through the turnstile with her coin and slipped her arms into the soft fur coat.

The other world looked different today. It had a different *feel* about it. She walked through a snowy field and listened to the crunch that her feet imprinted into the snow. She looked back to see her footprints, when all of a sudden, she saw Salvador Dali with a bull behind him in the distance. At the moment that he saw Dizzy turn to look at him, he waved a violet rag in front of the bull and it took off heading straight towards her. She ran as fast as she could and occasionally turned her head to see how close it was to her.

She was petrified and felt that it was sure to catch her up. Then she remembered the words of Phoebe, "Next time, turn around and ask the bull what it wants."

Dizzy felt some kind of strength, power through her body and she made a sharp halt and turned around. The bull, which was at arm's length, handed her a paint brush. Dizzy, with her mouth dropped, took the brush and thanked the bull. She walked away and the bull seemed to quietly walk away in the opposite direction. Dizzy felt the hairs on the back of her neck stand on end.

She walked a heart thudding walk through the snowy meadow, the paint brush clutched in her hand. It was early in the morning and she felt like the only human being in the world, although nature was making itself heard. Although she didn't know where she was, and there was no one to show her the way, she felt that she was walking in the right direction. She felt the weather getting warmer and took her coat off.

The sun was beaming and it began to feel more like a spring day. She had reached the top of a hill and wondered what might be on the other side of it. To her delight she saw the sea and she began to run down the hill to get to the beach. She ran and ran and thought that she saw someone on the beach who was waving to her. She got closer and closer and thought that her eyes might be playing tricks on her. She was wrong. It was her dad and tears started to well in her eyes as she panted towards him. He held his arms out to her and she ran and embraced him. They both laughed and cried together for a minute and Dizzy's deepest buried pain melted away.

They decided to paddle in the water, just like they used to when Dizzy was very young. Her dad would tell her that the waves were like white horses and they would jump together over each wave. The waves started to move fast, gushed towards them, and they jumped together and Dizzy felt truly *alive.* The force of the water felt like an immense strength, and jumping over the waves rather than running away from them felt exhilarating.

They walked a little further into the sea, making sure not to go too far out. Sea gulls were hovering over a certain spot on the water and Dizzy decided that she wanted to go and have a look. They waded out and saw something glimmering underneath the water. Dizzy could hardly believe her eyes. She saw words, floating in the water. Ordinary words, words that you would hardly think were important. Words like "but," "should," "could," "through," she read more, "another," "inspiring," "nevertheless," "wondered," "somewhere," "make," "urge," "alone," "enough," "curious," "discover," "into," "somehow," "something," "set forth," "there."

Dizzy felt dizzy with words and excitement. She decided to dip her hand into the water to see what word she would pull out, like when she played on the "lucky dip." She plunged her arm as deep as she could and closed her eyes. She dipped her brush under the water and hooked out the word *"yes."* Her dad grabbed and lifted her so that she would not sink.

Dizzy woke with the feeling that something had been revealed to her. She sensed that her mind and body held the knowledge of *something* that had previously been unknown. She was amazed at this other world that seemed to know much more than she did. She knew in her bones that it had a wisdom that was guiding her, helping her through her own destiny.

As she lay in bed she travelled back over the territory that she had been taken to in her dreams. She was becoming aware of something else that was pulling her towards painting. She knew that the upset of losing her dad had gouged a hole in her that had left her creative spirit lost, somewhere in limbo. It was like losing her favourite opal ring, the one that her dad had given her for her seventh birthday.

It had all started with her drawing a picture. A picture that was drawn and coloured without thinking, it had come from another part of her, an emotional part. Dizzy was connecting to something with which she had lost contact. The envy of others in school had also left her feeling empty and this had halted her growth. She had to follow her own form of education, one that came from within rather than one without.

CHAPTER 9

Today was a day of decisions. Deciding that from now on, she was going to paint her dreams anyway, regardless of what others thought. They would just have to accept it. She knew that she were being pulled by something that was a guiding force and her journey was an individual one, chosen for her.

She was quiet on the train journey back to Whitby. Her mum just thought that she was tired from the weekend and the bustle of London. She began to think of "journey" words that she liked, and the movement of the train helped her with this. "Starting," "halting," "advancing," "waiting," "destination," "arriving." She liked the rocking of the train and the way she could let her mind wander while it was going from place to place.

Finally, they pulled into Whitby station. Dizzy felt the comfort of her hometown. She loved the sea, the cobbled streets and the ancient feel of the old town and the ruins of the abbey on the hill. They picked up some fish and chips from their favourite chip shop and took them home. There was a sigh of relief and they both got into their slippers and pyjamas. They sat in the kitchen at the table and ate their supper; warmed by the food and contained by the homely kitchen atmosphere. There was a familiar seagull perched on the window ledge waiting for some scraps to eat. Dizzy saved a few chips and some batter and threw them out the window. There was a shriek of delight and with it, Dizzy felt truly at home. Today, there was nowhere else that she wanted to live.

It had been a long day, the journey had taken all day, but was worthwhile. Dizzy got a new little drawing pad that her mum had bought for her in the Tate gallery with some pencils. She started to draw a window...then the face of her dad with his comforting smile that told her that he loved her. She coloured the background in violet and sunk into her pillow and thought over the vision of her dad. She knew that the dream would support her for the rest of her life.

Her mum looked into the room and turned off the light. There was a presence in the room that was tangible. She knew that Dizzy was being looked after *somehow* and she respected her daughter's blessing.

Dizzy's sleep was deep and it wasn't long before she was *there* in her dream. She was in the back garden and in the distance she could see her dad smiling at her. She ran to him and he beckoned her to the sand pit, and they sat and played together. They arranged the sand objects and then made the outline of a flower in the sand. She carved out a centre of the flower and was happy with it. Then her dad put his hand into the centre and gently brushed some of the sand away. He took something out, it was small and shiny. He got rid of the sand from it and handed it to Dizzy. It was the opal ring that she had lost when he had died. She was so happy. She put the ring on and gave her dad a hug. She felt whole again, like a missing part of her had been found.

CHAPTER 10

Dizzy woke with a feeling of revelation. She got ready straight away and told her mum that she wanted to go into the garden. It was seven o'clock in the morning and a little unexpected but her mum let her go out and got some toast and tea ready for breakfast. Dizzy went to the sand pit and cleared the objects out of the way. She got her spade and started to *dig.* She moved faster and faster and her heart was racing. Further and further she dug, when at last she saw something glistening. She dug her nails into the sand and started to scrape away at it. She had found it, it was *there.*

She pulled the opal ring out and brushed away the sand. She was ecstatic. She ran back into the house calling her mum.

"Mum, I've found it, I've found my opal ring."

They both laughed and were overjoyed. It was her treasure that for so long she had *longed* for and had now found. They celebrated with hot chocolate and strawberries, Dizzy's favourite breakfast treat. Her mum washed the ring and *it dazzled once again.*

Dizzy sat at her desk. Finding the ring that glistened with colours inspired her to get out her paint box and brushes and make a picture in celebration. The return of the ring made her feel like she had found her soul again. She couldn't quite understand why it made such a difference to her, but it *did.*

Her mum had bought her a colour palette from the gallery and it was all shiny and new. She decided that she would *just* draw what came out naturally when she put pencil to paper. She started with two ears, then a round face. It began to look like an owl, so she drew two large eyes, a beak and set it in a small golden house. She looked at her paints and wondered what colour to paint the owl. She saw this as no ordinary owl, so she decided to colour it green. She didn't know why she wanted it to be green, but she *knew* that it *had* to be that colour. It felt fresh and full of new life. This time when she painted, she felt sure that *somewhere, somehow*, there was another presence helping her, guiding her.

The picture was carefully filled with the colours, but Dizzy thought that there was something missing. She pondered for a while. Then it came to her. She wanted *words* around the golden house. The words that she had seen just beneath the sea in the dream with her dad. Yes, that was it. So she got out her best ink pen and wrote all the words she could remember. These words, she thought, had travelled with her, guiding her to her destination.

She knew that "a picture could paint a thousand words" but came to realise that a thousand words could also paint a picture. There was something at work *behind* them, some kind of wisdom, mixing and transforming her. She felt that the images, together with the words of her dreams, would enrich her life in *this* world; weaving beautiful collages for her to paint. Once again, she would live in the playground of her imagination.

Dizzy looked at her opal ring and the brilliance of its colours. Reds, greens, blues and purples all sparkled as she stood next to her bedroom window, the sunlight resting on the stone. She knew that she would guard the ring with her life. She would *never* lose it again.